WIGGLESBOTTOM PRIMARY
THE SHARK IN THE POOL

THERE'S
LOADS MORE
MAYHEM IN

WigglesBottom PRIMARY
THE TOILET GHOST

WIGGLESBOTTOM PRIMARY
THE SHARK IN THE POOL

PAMELA BUTCHART

BECKA MOOR

nosy crow

WELCOME TO
WIGGLESBOTTOM PRIMARY!

MISS RILEY

HANA

LAUREN

JAYDEN

IRFAN

MEGAN

MILES

EVIE

SUSIE

MR HARRIS

SUNITA

ROZ

GAVIN

JOEL

ANNE-MARIE

BOBBY

THEO

First published in 2015 by Nosy Crow Ltd
The Crow's Nest, 10a Lant Street
London SE1 1QR

www.nosycrow.com

ISBN: 978 0 85763 481 8

Nosy Crow and associated logos are trademarks and/or registered
trademarks of Nosy Crow Ltd

Text copyright © Pamela Butchart 2015
Cover and inside illustrations © Becka Moor, 2015

The right of Pamela Butchart and Becka Moor to be identified
as the author and illustrator respectively has been asserted.

A CIP catalogue record for this book is available from the British Library.

Printed in Turkey by Imago

Papers used by Nosy Crow are made from wood grown in
sustainable forests.

3 5 7 9 8 6 4 2

CONTENTS

FOR LUCAS
AND ABBY
P. B.

FOR ROBERT
B. M.

THE SHARK
IN THE POOL

Last week during our swimming lesson Joel Jack started splashing and screaming so much that Mr Hobart (that's our swimming teacher) had to throw in the **EMERGENCY RING** and pull him to the side.

Once Joel Jack got out the pool he started rubbing his leg and shouting,

"I'VE BEEN BITTEN! THERE'S A SHARK IN THE POOL!!"

As soon as he said that **EVERYONE** started screaming and trying to get out of the pool and Mr Hobart had to blow his whistle **REALLY LOUDLY** to get us to stop.

Then Mr Hobart said, "Settle down! There are **NO** sharks in this pool. Now get back into your groups and follow the **POOL RULES!**"

So everyone settled down, except for Joel
Jack, who was lying at the side of the pool
with a towel over him.

When it was time for our Free Swim, we all swam over to where Joel was, and Sunita Ram said, "Joel. What do you think happened?"

Joel said that he didn't **THINK** anything. And that he **KNEW** what had happened. And that he had been the victim of a **SHARK ATTACK**!

So we asked if we could see his leg, and Joel said, "OK. But prepare yourself. It's not pretty."

And then he took a deep breath and pulled the towel off his leg. And that's when we all saw that Joel Jack **DIDN'T** have a bite mark and that his leg was just a bit red.

Once we got back to class, Sunita Ram told everyone at our table that Joel Jack **HADN'T** been bitten and that he was just being

DRAMATIC.

And that there weren't even any teeth marks.

But Joel Jack sits at the table **RIGHT** behind us so he heard **EVERYTHING**. And that's when he came over and pulled up his trouser leg and said, "Well, what do you call **THAT**?"

We all saw that the red mark looked a bit bigger than it had before, and also that there were lots of little dots inside it now.

Joel started pointing to all the little marks and counting them out loud. And that's when Irfan Baxter said that he thought the teeth marks looked too small to have been made by a shark, and that maybe Joel had been bitten by

PIRANHAS!

Then Irfan told us all about

PIRANHAS

and about how they are little fish with **TEETH** that bite people. And then he looked **REALLY CLOSELY** at Joel's leg, and said, "Yep. As I thought. Piranha bites."

The next week **NOBODY** would get into the pool because of the **PIRANHAS**. We all just stood at the side in our costumes.

Except for Susie Keys who was in the Deputy Head's office with Miss Riley because she'd given Miss Riley a note that said she was **ALLERGIC** to water, and also to piranhas, and said that her mum had written it.

But that was a **LIE** because everyone had seen her writing it herself in the changing rooms.

We all told Mr Hobart about the piranhas, but he didn't believe us. Even when Joel Jack showed him his leg, which was still all red, and Irfan showed him a picture of a brown piranha with a red tummy.

Mr Hobart said that it looked like Joel Jack had a rash, not a bite, and sent him to the nurse. Then Mr Hobart told us all to

WATCH CLOSELY

while he got the Big Net out and dragged it through the water, all the way from the Deep End to the Shallow End.

But even when Mr Hobart showed us that the net was empty, not even **ONE** person would go in the pool, in case the piranhas were hiding in the vents or sleeping at the bottom.

That's when Mr Hobart got so annoyed with us that he dived into the pool with his shorts and t-shirt on and swam underwater for **AGES** checking the Deep End, and all the corners, and the vents.

When he got out he said, "All clear! Now **PLEASE** get in!"

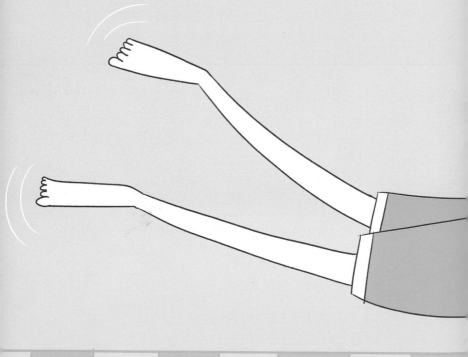

But we were still a bit unsure and I was worried because Mr Hobart hadn't been wearing goggles to look under the water, so I didn't think he would have been able to see properly.

But then Miss Riley came in with Susie Keys and she said, "If you don't all stop being silly **RIGHT NOW**, afternoon break will be **CANCELLED!**"

So everyone jumped in.

The swimming lesson didn't go very well because everyone was scared to swim too much in case we woke up the sleeping piranhas. And every time someone's leg accidently touched someone else's leg under the water people started screaming, so it was hard to concentrate on our Front Crawls.

Eventually Mr Hobart said there was no point trying to do the lesson any more, and that we all needed to learn to **RELAX** in the pool again. So he threw in all the fun stuff, like the floats and the tubes and the sinking weights.

After about a minute, **EVERYONE** had forgotten all about the piranhas and we were having the

BEST TIME EVER.

But when it was my turn to swim underwater and collect The Treasure, I thought I saw something brown floating near the Deep End. And then all of a sudden the floating thing got closer and

CLOSER

and even though I didn't have my goggles on I saw that it had a bit of red on its tummy and I **BURST** out of the water as fast as I could and screamed,

"PIRANHAAAAAAAAAA!"

Once Mr Hobart had finished telling us off for screaming and starting up all the "Piranha Nonsense" again, he showed us the Big Net and told us all to look inside.

I thought it might be a dead piranha. But it wasn't. It was a brown sticky-plaster with a bit of blood on it. Then Jayden King said, "Hey, that's mine! It must've fallen off in the pool."

And I realised that I **HADN'T** seen a piranha, and that I'd just seen Jayden King's knee plaster. But when we were walking back to class, Joel Jack came out of the nurse's room, and he ran up to me and Sunita and said, "Guess what?"

And we said, "What?"

And that's when he told us that the nurse had said Joel didn't have a bite on his leg and that it was just a nettle sting from playing Jungle Warriors in the grassy bit at break. And that the pool water must have made it hurt more and stopped it healing up properly. But then Joel stepped closer and looked around to make sure no one was spying on us. And then he said, "But I don't believe her, because it really stings!"

And then Joel Jack's eyes went **WIDE** and he said, "Can I tell you a secret?"

And we said yes.

And he said, "It's not a shark or a piranha in the pool. It's a **JELLYFISH!**"

DINOSAUR
BONES

One morning when our class were digging
holes for the tomato plants in the vegetable
garden, Gavin Ross found a **BONE!**

Everyone gasped when he held it up
because it was **HUGE!**

But then Miss Riley said, "Put that down, right away." And she made us all go back to the classroom and wash our hands twice.

EVERYONE kept asking Miss Riley, over and over again, about the bone but she just told us to concentrate on our reading and to forget about the bone.

But none of us could forget about the bone because it was

HUGE

and obviously a

DINOSAUR BONE!

At break time, Sunita Ram said that if it **WAS** a dinosaur bone then there would definitely be **MORE** bones. And then she said that the dinosaur was probably so

GINORMOUS

that the bone Gavin Ross found might only be the dinosaur's **PINKY TOE**.

Gavin said that he was going to do more digging and find more dinosaur bones. And Roz Morgan said that she was going to help, because she absolutely

LOVES dinosaurs

AND digging.

So that's when Gavin Ross and Roz Morgan

BROKE THE RULES

and went into the vegetable garden without permission.

Roz said that she was going to look for the dinosaur's **SKULL**, because she has over **SEVEN** dinosaur books and is a dinosaur **EXPERT**.

So Roz started digging at the opposite side
of the vegetable garden from where Gavin
had found the dinosaur's pinky-toe bone.
And then all of a sudden Gavin shouted,
"**LOOK AT THIS!**" And he'd found
LOADS of bones!

But then before Roz had a chance to find the skull, Susie Keys squealed, which we all knew meant a teacher was coming, because Susie was the **LOOK OUT**.

Roz jumped out of the vegetable garden really quickly, but Gavin was still climbing over the fence when Mr Harris got there, so he got a **DETENTION**.

That afternoon in class, Gavin Ross said that he didn't even **CARE** that he got a detention because soon he would be **FAMOUS** for finding the biggest dinosaur **EVER**.

But then the Deputy Head, Mr Harris, came into our classroom and told us all that the vegetable garden was

OUT OF BOUNDS

until the bones had been cleared away and it was safe again. And when Sunita Ram asked where the bones had come from, Mr Harris said that they were probably just bird bones. And that we weren't to worry about it.

So we all knew that Mr Harris hadn't actually **LOOKED** at the bones we had found because there was **NO WAY** they were bird bones. They were far too big!

45

At lunchtime, Gavin Ross called a secret meeting behind the recycling bins. That's when he told us that he thought Mr Harris was just **PRETENDING** that the dinosaur bones were bird bones because **HE** wanted to dig them up himself so that **HE** could be the one who became **FAMOUS** for finding the world's biggest dinosaur.

And we all agreed because it was obviously true.

So that's when Gavin said, "**I'M GOING BACK IN**." And also that he didn't care if he got **ONE HUNDRED** detentions.

Sunita Ram said that we needed to **CAMOUFLAGE** Gavin so that Mr Harris and the other teachers wouldn't be able to see him digging in the vegetable garden. So we all went over to the grassy bit and started kicking up mud and grass with our shoes like Sunita had told us to do. And then we used it to cover Gavin's face and hair and hands.

And Jayden King gave Gavin his coat to wear because it was brown with green on the arms, so it was perfect.

Everyone stood beside the Big Bush and watched Gavin climb over the fence and start digging.

Then Roz pulled one of her dinosaur books out of her bag **AND** the big dinosaur pinky-toe bone! And then she said that she had managed to grab it before Mr Harris could see. And that she'd hidden it in her bag.

And that's when I heard a little growling sound, but I just thought it was my stomach rumbling.

Roz began inspecting the dinosaur bone, and then looking at her book and shaking her head.

So we asked her what was wrong and she said that the bone didn't look like the ones in her book, and that this one didn't look old enough to be millions and millions of years old.

And then she said that you usually have to dig really,

REALLY

deep into the ground to find dinosaur bones, which didn't make sense because we hadn't been digging very deep at all, and we had only been using our hands.

Then Roz said that she wasn't sure if the bones **WERE** dinosaur bones any more. And that's when I heard the growling noise again. But this time it was **MUCH** louder. And it **DEFINITELY** wasn't coming from my stomach. It was coming from the Big Bush!

We all turned and looked and that's when we saw **TWO EYES** staring back at us! And I just **KNEW** that it was some sort of **BEAST**, and that the bones we found definitely **WEREN'T** dinosaur bones, and that they were probably the beast's **DINNER**!

And then someone shouted,

"It's a

WOLF!
RUN!"

And Roz dropped the big bone and we all ran to save Gavin as fast as we could.

But Gavin wouldn't stop digging up all of the wolf's bones so we shouted,

"STOP DIGGING, GAVIN! STOP!"

and we pointed back towards the Big Bush where the wolf was hiding.

And that's when the Big Bush started to shake. And we could hear growling all the way from the vegetable garden.

And then out jumped the **TINIEST DOG EVER!** And it grabbed the Big Bone in its mouth and started running towards us.

The tiny dog jumped **RIGHT OVER** the fence and dropped the bone into the hole with the other bones. And then it growled at Gavin a bit.

That's when the caretaker, Mr Poots, came out of his house and shouted, "**DAISY**! Get out of there!"

But Daisy just ignored him and began burying all the bones again.

And we all burst out laughing because Daisy definitely **WASN'T** a wolf.

Sunita Ram said that she thought Daisy had the littlest and angriest dinosaur face she'd ever seen, and everyone burst out laughing again because it was true.

Gavin Ross was really disappointed when we told him that the bones weren't dinosaur bones.

But then Daisy walked over and dropped something on Gavin's foot. It looked like one of those chocolate coins in gold foil you get at Christmas but I wasn't sure because of all the mud.

But then Gavin's eyes went **REALLY** wide.

And he said, "I can't believe it! Daisy found a **ROMAN COIN!**"

And everyone gasped!

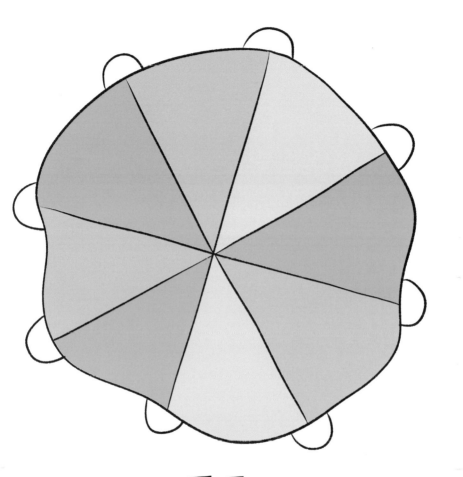

THE
PARACHUTE
OF
INVISIBILITY

Everyone in our class **LOVES** doing **PE** because we've got Miss Ranger and she's really fun and she lets our class do the **BEST** stuff because she says that we are mostly **WELL BEHAVED**.

Miss Ranger has a t-shirt with a PUG on it and that's why she's my best teacher because I **LOVE** pugs!

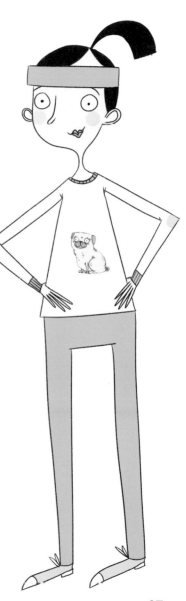

But one day when we came to do **PE**, Miss Ranger looked even more excited than she usually does.

That's when we saw the **PLAY PARACHUTE** piled up in the middle of the hall! We all started squealing and ran to the changing rooms, and that made Miss Ranger laugh.

Usually when we are getting changed we take too long, because it takes ages to get our tights off, and to tie our gym shoes, and to show each other all the stuff we have in our bags. But that day nobody said a **WORD** in the changing rooms and most of us ran out without even putting double knots in our laces. And Lauren Carr just put her t-shirt on over her shirt and kept her tights on.

We all helped Miss Ranger unfold the parachute because it was

HUGE!

Then Miss Ranger said, "Everyone make a big circle around the parachute." So we did.

Then Miss Ranger told us that the parachute was very **POWERFUL**. And that we should be **CAREFUL** and listen to her instructions closely.

And we all **GASPED** and **STARED** at each other when she said it, because none of us had realised that the parachute had actual **POWERS**!

Miss Ranger told each of us to pick up a bit of the parachute and start **SHAKING** it up and down to make waves, like the sea. And when we did it sounded like **THUNDER**! So that made us even **MORE** excited and Jayden King even screamed a bit.

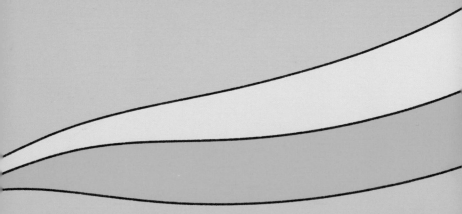

It got **REALLY** windy, and our hair was going all over the place, and everyone was screaming and laughing, and I couldn't even see Miss Ranger any more, and it felt like we were all in the middle of a great big

SEA STORM!

Then Miss Ranger shouted, "**THE WAVES ARE CALMING!**" and we knew that meant Miss Ranger wanted us to stop shaking the parachute up and down so much. But we didn't. We did it even

FASTER because it was fun.

But then Miss Ranger said,

"STOP, PLEASE!

Or I won't let you play the best game."

So we all stopped shaking the parachute right away.

Then Miss Ranger told us that we were going to create a

GIANT MUSHROOM

and all hide inside it!

Miss Ranger told us to lift the parachute up as **HIGH** as we could and then **RUN** into the middle and pull it under our bottoms and sit down. I didn't understand what was going to happen, but then Miss Ranger shouted,

"3-2-1 **GO!**"

So I just did it, and so did everyone else, and when we sat down the parachute stayed **UP**!

I didn't think it felt like we were inside a giant mushroom. I thought it felt like we were inside a hot air balloon! It was **BRILLIANT**!

But then Susie Keys gasped and whispered, "Where's Jayden?!" and I looked over and saw that Jayden wasn't sat next to Miss Ranger where he'd been before.

We looked around the circle and saw that he wasn't **ANYWHERE**. So Lauren Carr peeked out from the parachute but she couldn't see Jayden out there either. He'd **DISAPPEARED!**

And we all **KNEW** that it had happened because of the **POWERS** of the parachute!

Then Miss Ranger said it was time for our snack and told us all to pack up the parachute while she went to get the fruit bowl.

When we were folding the parachute Miles McKay kept shaking his head and saying, "Poor Jayden. It's our fault. Miss Ranger **TOLD** us to be careful, and we weren't."

He said that by **SHAKING** the parachute too much we had **ACTIVATED ITS POWERS**! And that the parachute must have done something to Jayden, like send him whizzing into space or turned him into dust!

Sunita Ram said that she thought Miles was right because we'd all heard Jayden scream, and now he had completely

VANISHED.

Then Miss Ranger called us over to the fruit bowl to get our snacks and as **SOON** as we got there **EVERYONE** gasped because we all saw that the **PEACH** was **GONE**! And Jayden **ALWAYS** runs to the fruit bowl first and takes the only peach because he **LOVES** them!

That's when Susie Keys said that she didn't think Jayden **WAS** in space **OR** that he'd been turned to dust, and that she thought the parachute had the power to turn people **INVISIBLE**. And we all **GASPED** because we knew she was right.

So everyone started shouting Jayden's name and we all walked around with our arms stretched out, trying to feel Jayden in the air around us.

But then we stopped because we heard slurping. And a peach stone rolled out from under the snack table and Miss Ranger lifted up the table cloth and Jayden came crawling out.

That's when Susie Keys rushed over to Jayden and told him that it was OK, and that the parachute's powers must have worn off, because we could see him again. And we all agreed. But Jayden looked a bit confused. And I didn't understand why he'd been under the table.

Then when we were walking back to our classroom, Jayden told me that the parachute **HADN'T** turned him invisible and that he'd got scared when everyone started shaking it so fast and had hidden under the table. He said that he thought everyone would laugh at him because he was scared of a parachute and that he wasn't

EVER

going to come out, but then he'd really wanted a peach.

So I promised that I wouldn't tell

ANYONE

that he'd been scared of the parachute. And I didn't.

And now it's really funny because sometimes we play a game where Jayden hides under the table, or in the store cupboard, and I pretend he's turned invisible again. And I'm **ALWAYS** the one who finds him first and **NOBODY** can work out why!

WIGGLESBOTTOM PRIMARY
THE TOILET GHOST

PTO for a SNEAK PEEK!

One time Gavin Ross asked to go to the toilet, and when he came back he was completely **SOAKED**.

That's when Miss Riley said, "What on **EARTH** happened to you, Gavin?"

And Gavin said, "Um. I don't know. I was just washing my hands, and then …

IT HAPPENED."

So Gavin got sent to the nurse to get changed, and when he came back he was wearing the spare "I-had-an-accident" clothes, and he wouldn't speak to **ANYONE**. We all thought the reason Gavin wouldn't speak to anyone was because the spare trousers were too short.

But then Theo Burke put his hand up and asked if he could go to the toilet and Gavin gasped!

That's when Gavin told us he thought the boys' toilets were **HAUNTED**. Because both taps had come on **FULL BLAST** even though he barely **TOUCHED** them!

But then Miss Riley came over and told us to stop chatting and to go back to our own tables. And then she tried to give the Toilet Pass to Theo Burke, but he said he didn't need to go any more, even though we all knew he did.

At break-time, we all ran outside and sat in the long grass. Sunita Ram said that we should all put our coats around Gavin's shoulders and take good care of him, because of the Toilet Ghost, so we did.